Santa's
World Map
1789

THIS IS A WAXCRAYON LTD BOOK

Text and design copyright © Waxcrayon Ltd 2013

Published in 2013 by Waxcrayon Ltd
18, Edinburgh Road, Freshwater, Isle of Wight PO40 9DL

A catalogue record for this book is available from the British Library.

ISBN-13: 978-0-9575770-3-9

Author: Russell Ince
Artwork: Russell Ince
Editor: Matt Sarson

www.santaclausthebook.com

Santa Claus

THE BOOK OF SECRETS

WRITTEN & ILLUSTRATED BY

RUSSELL INCE

December 2012

Dear Russell,

I am writing to kindly request your assistance with something of great importance.

We live in times of rapid change and with the arrival of the internet there may be an unlimited amount of information available to both children and parents alike. Whilst I see the arrival of this Wonderful new creation as a great step forward for Christmas, I also fill me with grave concern that the truth behind the story of Christmas and my part in it may be lost forever amongst the varying tales that appear online each year.

I have been watching you for some time now and can see that your skills as an illustrator and writer make you ideally suited to be able to help me. As such I am intrusting this journal to you in which I have recorded many of the secrets behind our operations here at the North Pole which have remained unrevealed for centuries.

I leave it to your best judgement as to what to do with this information and have faith in the fact that you will know how to best deliver my story to the world.

My best wishes to both you and your family.

Gratefully Yours

Santa Claus

Contents

Introduction

As a child, I was always blessed with the most magnificent Christmases. My parents love this time of year and so, without fail, it was magical in our home. It was not just about presents, but rather – the build–up, the decorating of the tree, the cooking and the preparation; all of the expectation and, of course, that lingering question: would Santa Claus visit?

I still remember, as if it was yesterday, one particular Christmas Eve when I was 7 or 8 years old. I had been lying on my bed for what seemed like hours, excitement keeping sleep at bay. It was then that I saw him; his face looking in through the crack between the curtains that hung from my first floor bedroom window. Santa Claus himself.

As a child, time seemed to slow almost to a stop at Christmas. The family was gathered in the house without anywhere to rush off to, nowhere else they had to be. We stayed in together, playing games and testing out that year's new toys.

As I grew older, Christmas only became even more magical. I have always found people are at their best over the festive period. You see the kindness of the human spirit shining through and the saying "Goodwill to all men" certainly seems to ring true, now more than at any other time.

Through my late teens and into adult life, my love of Christmas continued to grow stronger and stronger. I was blessed with the gift of meeting my now wife, Claire, who also shared my love of Christmas. We were married in December and visited Lapland for our honeymoon. It was the most incredible experience of my life, as here, in the fabled home of Santa Claus, amongst the snow covered plains, I found a magic and wonder that I never thought could be possible. It was here that I had my second personal encounter with the man himself.

It was evening and my wife and I had decided to go for a walk through the beautiful area around our cabin, where the snow rose up above our knees. As we strolled cautiously around a bend in the path, trying to keep our grip on the hard ice, the sight that met us left us spellbound. There, in a

single reindeer drawn sleigh, was Santa Claus. he was taking a nap, seemingly waiting for something or someone. We were so astounded by what we saw that we simply continued on our way, without even the softest of whispers. It was as if he was part of the scenery that should be left undisturbed.

Upon returning from our honeymoon, we decided that we would like to start our own Christmas business, something that would enable us to share our love of the festive period with the rest of the world, and soon we started making and selling decorations.

In the year 2012, I experienced my first Christmas as a father and, as such, it was the most magical yet. I woke up early on the morning of the big day, excited as ever, and went in to wake my daughter for her first ever Christmas. Arriving downstairs, I saw, resting on the mantelpiece above the fire, a beautifully wrapped gift with an envelope resting by its side. I assumed it was a present from my wife, placed there as a Christmas surprise. I would discover later, however, that my prediction was wrong. Upon picking up the letter, I soon realised that it was something very special. The beautifully scribed writing, the embossed red wax seal, my mind began to race with excitement. Could it be? Yes, it was. A letter from Santa Claus.

In the letter, he told me of how he could see that the modern world was changing so fast. The arrival of new things, such as the Internet and films, meant that children now had access to so much information that he was worried the real truth about Christmas might be lost forever. As such, he had left me a journal containing knowledge that had remained a closely guarded secret for centuries. he said that, as an illustrator and writer who kept Christmas alive in my heart all year round, I would know what to do with it and as such help spread the truth about Christmas to the children of the world.

So here it follows, the truth behind one of the world's oldest and greatest mysteries, in the words of Santa Claus himself. I have tried my best to do such an important story justice, and hope that you enjoy reading it.

Russell

History

Many centuries ago, I was known to people simply as Nichlaus, or Nicholas, depending on which country you were from. I lived in a small wooden house with my wife and was blessed with the ability of being able to make anything I desired out of wood, with toys being my personal favourite. Only the wealthier people could afford to spend money on luxuries such as toys and so I had to make all sorts of different things.

Having seen the joy that my toys brought to the children of those who were lucky enough to be able to afford them, I could not bear to think that the majority of children in my village were going without. As such, throughout the year, I would make wooden toys and my wife would sew dolls, whenever we had a spare evening.

Upon the Eve of Christmas, I would ride through the village in my sleigh and deliver these toys to all of the children, even those whose families could not afford to buy their own. I did this for many years, until my beard grew white and the twilight of my life began to descend.

History has, at times, got me confused with many great people around the world, such as the famous bishop of Lycia (now in Turkey), St Nicholas. I am afraid that this is not so, I am still and have always been just a humble toymaker.

In a time when humans were living the early chapters of their story on earth and for thousands of years before that, magic was as commonplace and as accepted as the wind and rain, and many magical races shared the planet. At first, humans were just another race

of creature who called Earth their home and they were able to accept their magical neighbours, despite not always seeing eye to eye. This is well documented in the old tales and myths, still told in many countries today.

As the human population grew and villages began to move to new lands in search of a better life, confusion and distrust seemed to spread along with them, leading to many of the ancient beings having to go into hiding.

Now, whilst their numbers have decreased radically, I can certainly state with confidence that these magical people still exist. Why am I so sure? Well let me tell you. One Christmas Eve, as I was finishing my annual rounds, I found myself confronted by a group of very small people who appeared to be Elves. They greeted me politely and went on to tell me of how they sensed the early signs of the downfall of man and, realising that the fate of both Elf and human were entwined together, knew that something must change. The high Council of Elven Elders had foretold that it must be one of humanity's own who brought hope and salvation.

Needless to say, my wife and I were astonished by what was happening and, in our state of shock, seemed able to do nothing other than simply follow these wondrous little people. The snowstorm, through which we found ourselves travelling for hours, suddenly cleared, as quickly as it had arrived, and before us lay a mysterious village. here, I was told that I had been chosen to continue the work I had already begun and that I would deliver gifts to the children of the entire world.

Job & Duties

Once at the village, we were taken to see the high Council of Elven Elders – a circle of the oldest and wisest Elves. Here they explained to me their vision of Santa Claus and how it would be the job of both Santa and the Elves to serve the good of all mankind.

It was foreseen, that by delivering toys to the children of the world on one special night of the year, hope, happiness and love would spread across the globe. This would capture the hearts of mankind, with enough power to last the whole year through. Because it is always children who hold the key to the future in their hands, it was decided that they would be the ones to receive gifts. To bring joy to a child was thought to be the most magical of things for Elves, for, as the old Elven saying goes, "When a child smiles, the whole world smiles with them."

I learned that the Elves had been watching me for many years and that I had shown myself worthy of becoming Santa Claus. If I were to take the job, my wife and I would go to live with the Elves in their village and be rewarded with the same long lives that they have. In return for this opportunity, we must dedicate the rest of our days to the service of Christmas and the spreading of goodwill to all men.

The Elven Elders, when deciding that a human should be the one to bring hope to the world, gave several extremely rare and precious gifts. These were to assist whoever was to become Santa Claus in spreading magic, joy and hope across the world and I will tell you more of these later.

How could I possibly deny myself the opportunity of doing what I loved the most and, in doing so, spread the spirit of giving and happiness around the entire world? From that day forth, I have been known as Santa Claus.

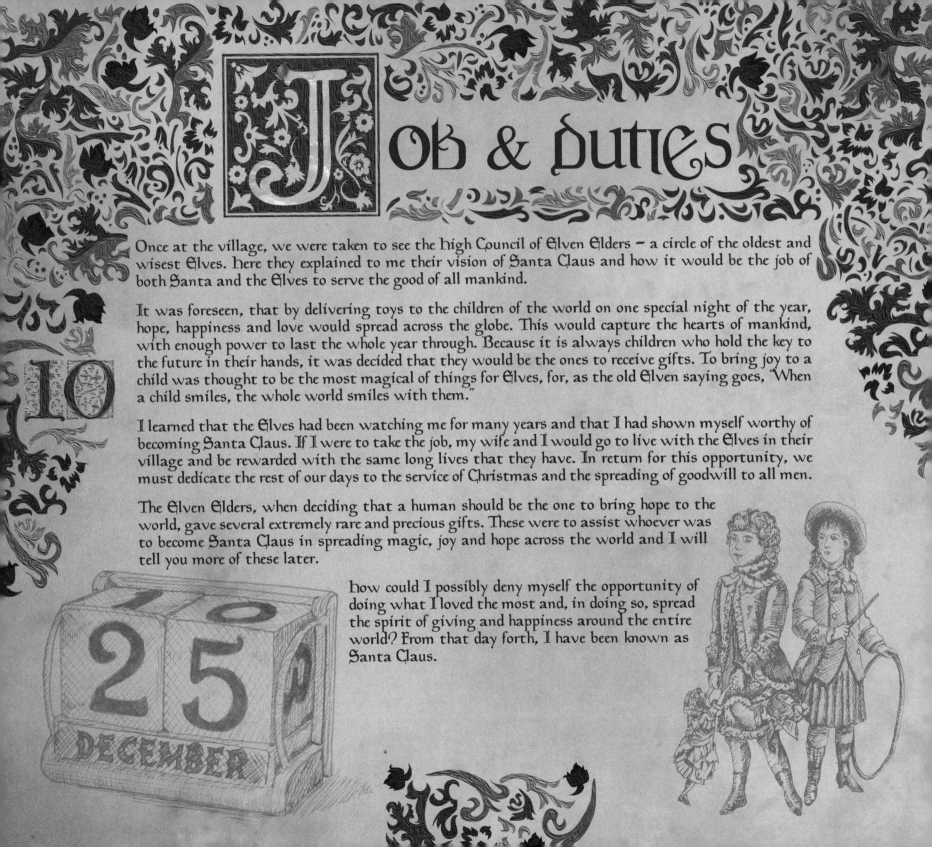

# NORTH POLE

The curious village at which we had somehow arrived, whilst both beautiful and magical in its white splendour, seemed to be in the most barren and lonesome place on Earth. Whilst I am unable to tell you its exact location, I can say that it was somewhere in what is now known as Northern Finland.

As I mentioned earlier, the migration of humans had driven the magical peoples deeper and deeper into hiding and, thus, to more and more remote areas. After a hundred years, or thereabouts, it was determined that in order to keep the village a secret, we would have to move. It was decided that we should relocate to a place now known as Greenland. At this time nobody at all lived there, it was snowy and cold in the winter and green and cold in the summer.

Eventually, humans began to explore and push the boundaries of their world further and further, and so again came the time to protect our operation and move on once more. Looking to the future and seeing what might come to pass, it was decided that the only place left for us was somewhere so remote that humans would never venture there. It would need to be very hard for them to survive the conditions and would offer nothing of any value...The North Pole.

It was the perfect location for many reasons. It was inaccessible, due to the icy landscape and harsh weather conditions. At the time, the polar region was completely uncharted territory; there were no maps, for no human had ever been there. As the ice is constantly moving, our village would never be in the same place for more than two days in a row. Today the village may be to the West of the Pole and tomorrow it may be to the South. Something else that still continues to protect our village to this day is that it is hidden behind moving ice ridges and a swirling cloud of icy fog. This makes it almost impossible to spot from either land or air.

Helpers

It was not too many years after taking on my role as Santa that I began to realise that even with the marvellous community of Elves, if we were going to do our job to the best of our ability, we were going to need help.

The problem we faced was that neither the Elves nor myself were in a position to personally take care of things out in the wider world. I had too many other duties to fulfil and the Elves looked too different to be able to blend into human society.

When we needed information about new addresses, maps and news of which toys had been the most popular the previous Christmas, we found that we were just too isolated up at the North Pole. We were also concerned that too many comings and goings would risk revealing the location we had worked so hard to conceal.

As the human world grew, it became ever more complicated. Little settlements became villages, villages became towns and towns became cities. Our helpers first started out as just the odd good-hearted and trustworthy individual. Soon teachers and toyshop owners were recruited and, over the years, many more people were required to help. If someone shows themselves to be pure of heart, with a particular skill that could be of service, they may be offered the chance to become a helper and work with the Elves and myself.

Today, our network spreads right across the globe. There are literally thousands of helpers from all walks of life, such as — weathermen, policemen, soldiers, air traffic controllers and postmen, even Presidents and Prime Ministers. Without the help of all these people, who secretly go about their work, Christmas would not exist as we know it and I would not be able to carry out my duties as Santa Claus.

Post Office

The creation of the network of helpers brought about another requirement; the ability to communicate. How would the helpers from around the world get their information to us? And equally how would we contact them? You must remember that this happened in a time long before the Internet or even telephones existed, and hundreds of years before the first official postal service.

The Elves, as always, came up with a rather splendid solution and soon we had created a very special post office. Each helper was issued with a magic postage stamp, which, once inked and printed on paper, if left by a chimney or open window, would be collected by the wind and carried all the way to the North Pole.

The letters would then make their way across oceans and continents, until finally reaching the large chimney at the post office. They would then be read by the Head Post Elf and passed on to the appropriate department within the village.

You may be wondering; "How does this magic work?" Whilst my many years have enabled me to learn much, there are still aspects of the Elven secrets that I do not understand and, therefore, I am afraid I can tell you no more about the magic postal winds, than you could about the inner workings of the Internet. I do know, however, that the postage stamp sends a signal to the post office, which triggers the "magic winds" to trace and collect the letter.

As the centuries passed and gradually more people began to read and write, the network of helpers informed us that children wanted to send us letters of thanks for their toys, but did not know where to send them. It was decided that the same magic that worked with the special postage stamp, would be expanded to recognise any letter addressed to "Santa Claus."

Soon, word began to spread that letters addressed to Santa Claus (or any of the other names I am known by) would make their way to me on the magic winds and, as such, each year, more and more children began to write.

Letters

As the centuries rolled by and increasing numbers of children learned to write, more and more began to send letters to me.

Firstly, they wrote only letters of thanks, but then, as the season of Christmas approached, many began asking for specific gifts and toys. At first I was a little surprised by this, but I soon realised that if I could give a child something they wanted, rather than just what we chose for them, it could only be a positive thing.

Today, with so many children being able to read and write, sending a letter before Christmas, asking for gifts and toys, has become a tradition for boys and girls everywhere. Each year, the magical postage system sees millions of letters collected from fireplaces, windows and homes all over the world. Upon arrival they are all read, sorted and passed on to the appropriate department within the village.

I do like to reply to as many letters as I can, but, as I am sure you can imagine, it is not possible for me to answer each of the many millions of letters I receive, in such a short period of time. So, even though you may not receive an answer from the North Pole, I can promise that your letters do always arrive safely, are read very carefully and any requests noted down.

If you would like to write to me, it is very easy. Write your letter – your parents can help if you like – seal it in an envelope and make sure that it is addressed to me, at the North Pole. Leave the letter out when you go to bed. It is best by a fireplace, but if you do not have one, next to a window, on a table or anywhere out in the open will do. If you would rather, just pop it in a post box, it will always find its way to me.

Naughty & Nice

I know that it has long been debated, how I monitor and decide which children have been naughty and which have been nice.

Everyone knows that only those children who make it onto the nice list receive a visit from me on Christmas Eve. However, it has not always been this way. When I first began making toys for the children in my village, and during my early years as Santa Claus, every child was given a toy. It was Mrs Claus who pointed out that maybe this was not fair. She felt that only those children who had been good should be rewarded with a gift. Having thought very carefully about this, I finally agreed with her. From that year on, I chose to only visit those children who were nice.

When the new rule was first introduced, it was difficult for the helpers to keep track of every child's behaviour. The Elves set about solving this problem with a little of their magic. When each child is born they are given their own pigeonhole, which is like their own personal shelf in the hall of records. On each shelf, there is a Year Glass, which looks just like a sand timer. These Year Glasses are made with Elven magic and are tuned to each individual child. Throughout their lives, every time a child does something good the sand grains move to the nice side and every time they do something bad, sand travels over to the naughty side. Each year when it is time to produce the lists of naughty and nice children, those with more sand on the nice side of the Year Glass go on to the nice list and those with more sand on the naughty side go on the naughty list.

So, the secret to making it on the nice list each year is very simple. Make sure that you do more nice things than naughty things.

Elves

From what I can tell, it seems that the world has developed a very clear picture of who the Elves are and what they look like. Much of that seems to be correct, but there are some important details that I feel you should know:

- Elves are very happy people; they are very rarely sad. They are also extremely kind and love to give and to share.
- Elves are very short compared to most adult humans, being around three and a half to four feet tall.
- Elves' ears come to a point at the top.
- Elves have what you might call magic, but it is in fact more of an ancient understanding of nature and how the world works.
- Elves live much, much longer lives than humans, even hundreds and hundreds of years.
    - Elves' favourite foods are gingerbread and Brussels sprouts.
    - Elves need very little food compared to humans, due to the fact that their bodies work slightly differently.
    - Elves love to work and make things; taking great pride in everything they do.
    - Elves have a better understanding of time than we do. To them a day can be as long as a week and, because of this, they are never, ever late.

As I wrote at the beginning of this book, it was the Elves who created the role of Santa Claus and were kind enough to offer me the job. Whilst Mrs Claus and I have been involved for hundreds of years now, without the Elves, Christmas would never have become the magic-filled festival that it is today.

It is said that Elves are just one of the many original magical races that called Earth their home, long before us humans arrived. Elves lived all across what is now known as Northern Europe, in the areas that today form the countries – Norway, Sweden, Finland, Denmark, England, Ireland, Scotland and Germany. They lived here mainly due to their love of the colder weather and, of course, thousands of years ago, Northern Europe was much colder than it is today.

Over the many centuries that they have shared Earth with humans, Elves have tried their best to help us, even though we sometimes do horrible things. They love all plants and animals, and their ancient wisdom means that they have long known that the health of our planet depends on the balance and protection of everything in nature. This is part of the reason why they created the idea of Santa Claus. They knew that humans were growing in number and would someday hold the future in their hands. They thought that by bringing hope and magic into the world, and reminding us of the warmth of sharing and giving, it might, in some way, prevent us from choosing the wrong path.

At first, humans settled near to Elven villages, existing happily side-by-side, but time seemed to change this relationship. Eventually, afraid of living too close to their new neighbours, the Elves began to withdraw into hiding, which is where they still remain today.

Santa's Village

Although "Santa's Village" is the name given to it around the world, it is no more my village than anyone else's. The village exists to benefit all of mankind and is built on a foundation of love for the children of all nations. As long as the village exists, it will be here to serve the world.

The village itself is at the heart of our North Pole location. Whilst the vast majority of it lies hidden beneath the ice, for the benefit of both insulation against the cold and camouflage, it is unavoidable that a certain amount exists out in the open air.

With the arrival of air travel and more frequent flights, we could no longer rely on our remote location to remain a secret. We had to take steps to secure the village, and now icy crags and thick swirling fogs protect it.

The village is much the same as any other. It has a baker, a tailor, a cobbler and many other shops, all built around a large marketplace. There is, however, one main difference to the villages you are probably familiar with — at the North Pole we do not use money. Everything at the market and in all of the shops is free. Each Elf makes his or her contribution to life here, whilst taking only what they need and no more. Those who are good at making toys, make toys, those who are good cooks, make food, and so on. This way, each Elf has everything that they need to live a nice, comfortable life, without having to worry about paying for anything.

It is important to understand that we are cut off from the rest of the world up here and if we need something, most of the time we have to make it ourselves. It is not quite so easy to buy things, and there is certainly no Internet shopping.

Some of the most important places in Santa's Village are — the post office, toy factory, Elves' houses, Santa's house, reindeer stable, Elf school, sleigh garage, library, husky kennels, town hall and the hall of records.

18

Welcome to
Santa's Village
North Pole

Santa's House

I see that there are many different ideas of how my house looks and where I live. The simple truth is that I live in a small wooden cabin, just outside of the main village at the North Pole.

With just Mrs Claus and myself living there, we do not have the need for very much. The house sits on one floor and has a very simple, but well-appointed kitchen, with a big open fireplace, cast iron stove and a wooden dining table and chairs. We have a small, but cosy bedroom with a very special Elven-made bed. Upon this sits a large, thick patchwork quilt, which keeps us nice and warm at night. There is also a bathroom with a sauna in it, which is quite wonderful for thawing out after being exposed to the bitterly cold weather outside.

The final room is the library. Here I have a large desk and all around dark wooden bookcases, which run from the floor all the way up to the ceiling. It is here that I keep some of the scrolls, maps and books that I have collected over the many years. The library is where I spend most of my time when at home. I have a comfortable, leather armchair and can often be found here in the evenings, reading in front of the crackling, warm glow of the fireplace.

In reality, I do not often get to spend much time in the house, as there is always a list of important duties to be seen to around the village. The house has changed very little over the years, as it is a retreat for Mrs Claus and I. It is a place where we can escape the hustle and bustle of both the modern world and the North Pole, and enjoy the simple pleasures of life, such as a good book and a warm home cooked meal.

19

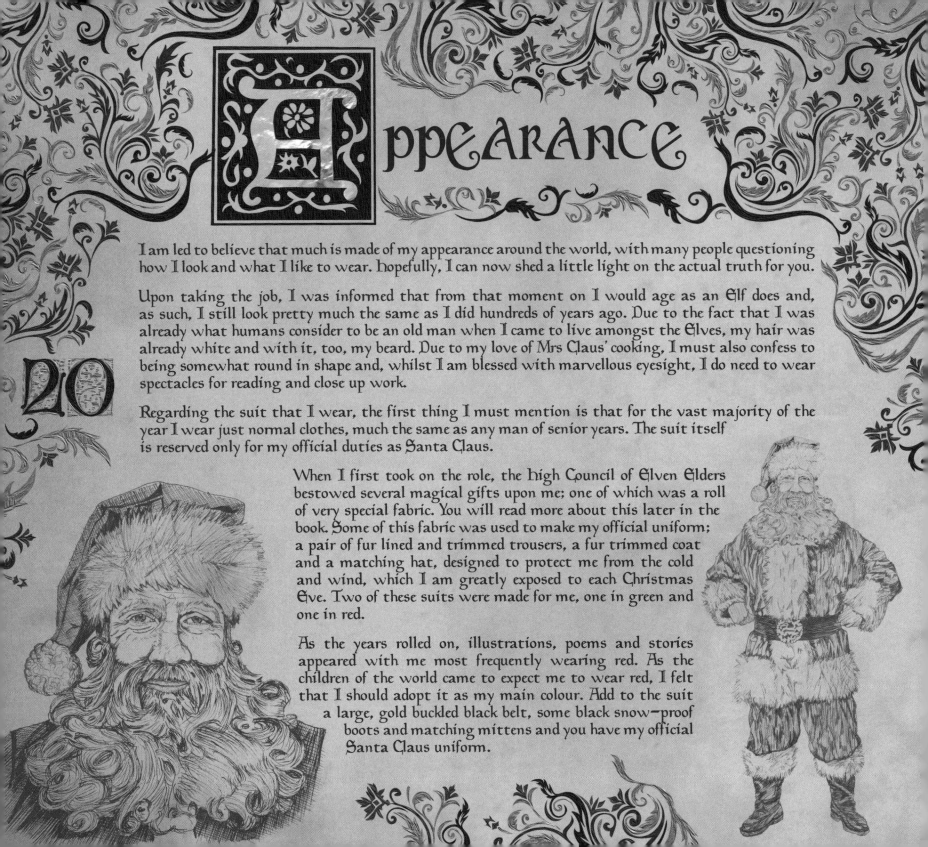

Appearance

I am led to believe that much is made of my appearance around the world, with many people questioning how I look and what I like to wear. Hopefully, I can now shed a little light on the actual truth for you.

Upon taking the job, I was informed that from that moment on I would age as an Elf does and, as such, I still look pretty much the same as I did hundreds of years ago. Due to the fact that I was already what humans consider to be an old man when I came to live amongst the Elves, my hair was already white and with it, too, my beard. Due to my love of Mrs Claus' cooking, I must also confess to being somewhat round in shape and, whilst I am blessed with marvellous eyesight, I do need to wear spectacles for reading and close up work.

Regarding the suit that I wear, the first thing I must mention is that for the vast majority of the year I wear just normal clothes, much the same as any man of senior years. The suit itself is reserved only for my official duties as Santa Claus.

When I first took on the role, the High Council of Elven Elders bestowed several magical gifts upon me; one of which was a roll of very special fabric. You will read more about this later in the book. Some of this fabric was used to make my official uniform; a pair of fur lined and trimmed trousers, a fur trimmed coat and a matching hat, designed to protect me from the cold and wind, which I am greatly exposed to each Christmas Eve. Two of these suits were made for me, one in green and one in red.

As the years rolled on, illustrations, poems and stories appeared with me most frequently wearing red. As the children of the world came to expect me to wear red, I felt that I should adopt it as my main colour. Add to the suit a large, gold buckled black belt, some black snow-proof boots and matching mittens and you have my official Santa Claus uniform.

Toys & Gifts

Despite all the years that have passed since I was fortunate enough to become Santa Claus, I still consider myself, at heart, to be a toymaker.

When I first began delivering presents and gifts, many centuries ago, the inhabited world was a much smaller place, with nowhere near the number of children that there are today. For centuries the children of the world were delighted by toys and games made from colourfully painted wood and soft fabrics. Providing endless entertainment, these simple toys, when combined with a little imagination, enabled the exploration of the furthest realms of possibility.

Today, the world is almost unrecognisable to that of yesteryear. Technology has achieved heights that I could never have foreseen; computers, games consoles and remote control toys all lead today's market. Whilst the toys of years-gone-by may appear to be completely different to the electronic masterpieces of nowadays, they are still, essentially, the same thing. They provide endless hours of fun and laughter to children, enabling their imaginations to carry them away on adventures that know no bounds.

So, how does toy making actually work? Well, you may be surprised to know that nearly all toys made in the world start their lives here, at the North Pole. The Elves have always been the greatest of inventors and that is still the case today. However, it is not possible to produce enough toys for every child in the world without help. Each of the major toy manufacturers has at least one very important staff member who is an official helper of Santa Claus.

In return for helping with the sourcing of materials and creation of components, toy companies are allowed to put Elven designs into production and sell them all year round. Making enough toys for the whole world to buy throughout the year would be very difficult to do from the North Pole alone. By working together, we can make the best quality toys for the largest number of children and, in doing so, make sure that I am able to complete my rounds on Christmas Eve.

Santa's Year

JANUARY:

I tend to rest and try to recover from the extreme efforts of December. I only take on light duties, such as looking after the reindeer.

FEBRUARY:

I review the toys and presents from the previous year to see how successful we have been in our duties. We also consult the major toy companies to see what is likely to be popular in the coming year.

MARCH:

The reindeer begin their training, after a couple of months of well-earned rest. We also hold trials to see whether any new recruits are ready to join our Christmas teams.

APRIL:

This month is all about spring-cleaning – my house, the library, the post office and the factory. In fact, everything gets a good scrub. Last year's letters, lists and reports are all filed and space is made for the coming year's work. Valuable documents in the library are checked and cleaned if necessary. We also service and oil all of the machines and tools in the factory and workshops to make sure that they are ready for the coming peak production period.

MAY:

You might be surprised to hear that May is probably the most important month of the year for Christmas. This is the month that I must travel alone, through the barren landscape of the North, to visit the high Council of Elven Elders. We discuss many things: the previous year and my plans for the coming Christmas; what is happening in the world at large; how children are changing and whether the Elves and myself have done a good job. It is only with the blessing of the Elders that I am granted permission to carry on my work each year.

JUNE & JULY:

I like to travel the world, along with Mrs Claus, in full disguise. We offer help to people in need, look for potential new helpers and spend some time to ensure that we keep in touch with the world and all of its changes. I stay in hotels, go to the cinema, fly in aeroplanes, read books, eat in restaurants and, sometimes, I even get a part-time job.

AUGUST:

I always need to catch up with what I have missed, whilst we were away. I have lots of meetings with the head Elf and the Elves who are in charge of various operations, both in the Village and around the world. I like to hear about any problems that may have occurred, exciting new things that have happened and new toys that have been produced. It is now that things really start gaining momentum, as the Christmas season begins.

SEPTEMBER:

This month is all about navigation. I start planning my journey for Christmas Eve, and check the latest flight times and routes. I also plan and map the checkpoints, where I will be loaded up with a new batch of presents.

OCTOBER:

Letters start to come in from all over the world. From this moment on, I spend a lot of my time in the post office, reading letters and helping to keep a record of all the children's requests.

NOVEMBER:

It is now time to review the Year Glasses and write up the annual naughty and nice lists. We complete a factory stock check, just to make sure that we have enough toys. I also service the sleigh and get it ready for the long journey ahead.

DECEMBER:

The busiest month of all is taken up with so many jobs, it is impossible to list them all. They include – preparing the reindeer team, final checks of the naughty and nice lists and my Christmas Eve route and wrapping up all the presents.

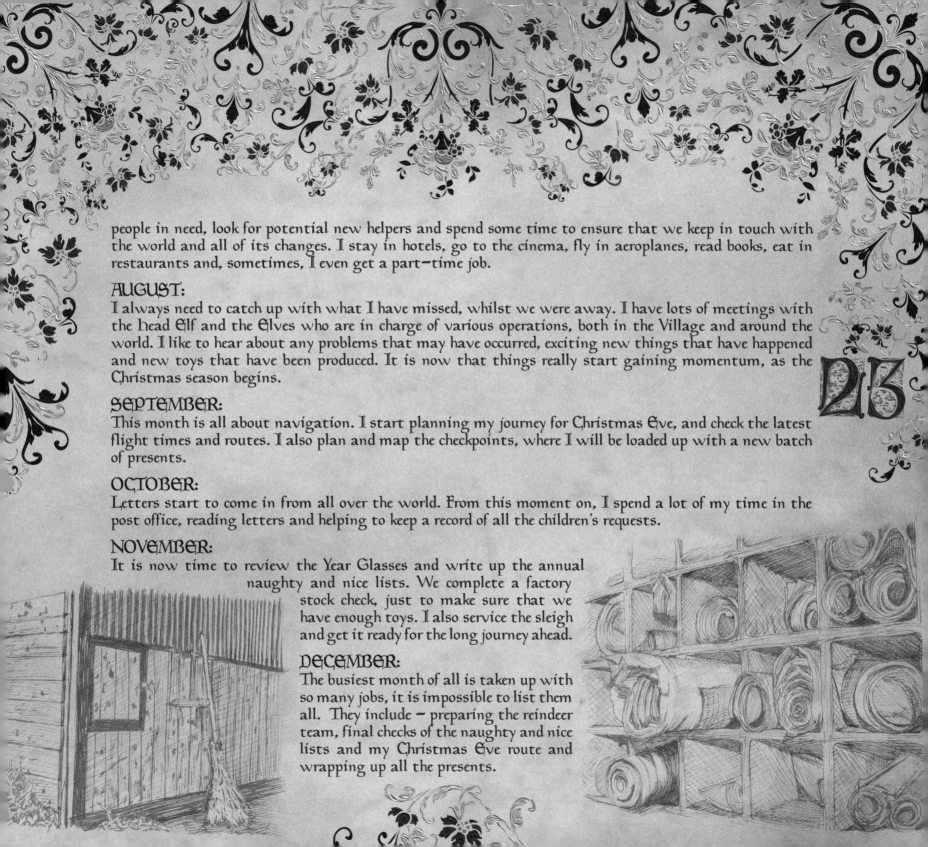

Reindeer

I am aware that my very special team of reindeer have become one of the most recognisable images associated with Christmas. Whilst most people seem to know that the reindeer fly me around the world each Christmas Eve, I feel that now is the right time to reveal the secret of how it happens.

There is one particular type of reindeer, whose unique talents led to them being invited to help the Elves at Christmas. Peary reindeer have always lived in remote areas, at the very top of the world and, as such, their remarkable bodies have adapted, over thousands of years, to help them survive even the most harsh and dangerous of conditions.

One of the main hazards facing the reindeer are the deep cracks and crevices that regularly appear in the constantly moving ice. The Peary are extremely fast and have unique antlers that act like small aeroplane wings. These factors, in combination with their incredible muscles and tendons, enable this little reindeer to leap to extraordinary heights. This ability to leap is aided by their remarkably light bones and feather-like fur, helping them to stay in the air for prolonged periods of time.

Posing another major threat to the reindeer are the almighty snowdrifts, which often occur at the North Pole. To help them escape deeper snow, the Peary have a leather-like web between the two "toes" of their hooves, which they use to pull themselves through the snow, in a similar way to how ducks move through water.

Whilst you may be surprised to hear that reindeer cannot fly in the same way that a bird does, I hope that you still understand how valuable their role is, using their speed and immense leap to launch the sleigh into the air. Their antlers and the webs of their feet then help to pull and steer the sleigh through the air, land and take off again. Over the centuries my reindeer have never let me down and, despite the temptation to use modern technology to assist me, I, at least for now, see no reason to change things.

SLEIGH

As I mentioned earlier, when I was first taken by the Elves to their village and asked if I would like to take on the role of Santa Claus, by the High Council of Elven Elders, they gave me several magical gifts. Another of these gifts was the wood cut from an extremely rare and magical tree, which grows deep in a mystical, remote forest. This wood was used to make the sleigh, which has, each year, taken me around the world to deliver presents, century after century.

I was informed that once complete, the sleigh would fly with the help of a special team of reindeer. Of course, initially I laughed at the idea of flying a sleigh. However, it was then explained to me that trees find it very hard to survive in snowy conditions and, if the seeds are able to travel long distances in the wind, it improves the chance of the rare trees surviving. They do this by drawing gases from the soil and air, which then fill the seeds and, later, the wood itself with little pockets of these gases. This then acts in much the same way as the gas in a helium balloon does.

The wood was carved and, with the help of some Elven magic, the sleigh was made and, finally, painted. It is relatively simple compared to modern day flying machines; it has a nice comfortable bench seat in front of an open back compartment, which is large enough to hold multiple sacks of presents. In front of the seat is a small compartment, where I store my maps, and a rack to hold the reindeer's reins.

Whilst it may seem complicated, it really is quite simple; the reindeer use their amazing speed, followed by their giant leap and aeroplane wing like antlers to help the sleigh take off. The sleigh then takes over the flying and the reindeer just help to steer, land and take off once more.

Food & Drink

Believe it or not, the tradition of leaving food out for me began even before Santa Claus existed. Back in the time when I would just deliver toys to the children in my village, many of the parents wanted to pay me, but, as I already knew, most could not afford to. Because people back then mainly grew or caught all of their food themselves, they began to give me food instead of money. After all, Christmas was and still is a time for celebration and feasting. I would receive jams and preserves, vegetables, cuts of meat, pies and many other things that folk were kind enough to share.

After I accepted the role of Santa Claus, the idea of leaving food as a thank you gradually spread around the world. However, it is not possible for the reindeer and I to eat all of the food left out for us, at the millions of homes that we visit. Living at the North Pole, which is snow and ice all year round makes it very difficult to grow fruit, vegetables or crops of any kind. One of the benefits of the icy conditions is that it acts as one big, natural freezer and, because of this, it is splendid for storing food and making sure that nothing ever goes to waste.

Nowadays, almost every house I visit leaves food and drink out for the team of reindeer and myself, which is always a welcome sight on such a long night. The tradition of what food to leave out varies greatly, depending on the country I am visiting. To name just a few: In England it is mince pies and sherry; Denmark – rice pudding; Chile – a candied fruit sponge cake; Japan – a Christmas cake covered in cream and strawberries; Sweden and Norway – porridge; Ireland – Guinness and, of course, in the USA, it is milk and cookies.

I would like to take this opportunity to say thank you for the lovely food and drink that you leave, whatever it may be. The Elves, reindeer and myself are always very grateful.

Chimneys

I know that one of the biggest mysteries surrounding Christmas Eve has always been how I get into the houses to leave the presents.

Well, there is not just one simple answer. Over the centuries, houses have changed a lot, as back when I first began, the majority were just simple huts. They gradually became larger and began to be built from stone and brick; extra floors were added, as were fireplaces, chimneys and glass windows. More recently, when houses in colder regions began to add central heating, many people started to block up their chimneys, which once again changed everything.

The secret as to how I have managed to enter houses over the centuries, for the most part undetected, lies in another gift that I received from the Elven Elders. Along with the wood for the sleigh, I was given a long roll of cloth, woven from magical fibres. As you know, this roll of cloth was used to make my official Santa suit, it was also used to make my toy sacks. The cloth has the ability to make whatever it contains shrink down much smaller than its original size. This means that, when I make my visits on Christmas Eve, I am able to fit thousands of toys into one sack. Also, the suit enables me to transform into what I can only describe as a "wisp of wind" and pass through any small gap, from a chimney to a keyhole.

Each year I am allocated a certain amount of magic to use during the Christmas period, but once it is all used up, there is no more until the next year. It is like a battery filled with magic and, once the battery is flat, it no longer works. A lot of this magic is used up in flying around the world and getting in and out of people's houses.

If you are able to leave a magic key hanging out for me on Christmas Eve it will save me from having to use up some of my vital reserves.

Christmas Eve

Christmas Eve is the one night of the year that all of us at the North Pole look forward to. It is the night that my team of reindeer and I fly around the world delivering presents to all of the good boys and girls.

I always rise early on Christmas Eve, check on the reindeer and go over my route maps, which are carefully arranged to accommodate aeroplane flight paths and all of the different time zones. The Elves are responsible for making sure that all of the gifts are packed in their sacks. When it is time to leave, the reindeer are hitched up to the sleigh and the first load of the gifts are stowed on board. Only then can the magical journey begin.

I know that a lot of people wonder how I manage to fly around the whole world in just one night. Whilst it is not easy, I will do my best to explain how time seemingly travels with me.

The first thing that you must remember is that it is not night in every country at the same time. For example, when it is light in Europe, it is dark in Australia. I fly, following night around the world.

Most people live in countries situated on the top half of the globe, known as the Northern hemisphere. Christmas falls at the time of year when days are at their shortest and nights at their longest in this half of the world, which means that I have more hours of darkness to complete my journey at Christmas, than at any other time of the year.

How is it possible for me to complete all of these deliveries in just one night? This question was one of the things that I did not understand when I first became Santa Claus. The Elves taught me that time itself is not as humans choose to measure it. Instead of time occurring in a straight line, where one hour follows another and then another, time is in fact more like many layers of circles, one on top of the other. This makes it possible to slow down the passing of time, simply by moving from one circle to another. This fact is also behind the secret of how the Elves, and now myself and Mrs Claus, enjoy much longer lives.

Now you know that I am able to follow the shadow of night, as it slowly makes its way around the world and that I make use of ancient Elven knowledge, in order to slow down the passage of time. All this leaves is the question of how I am able to fit enough toys for all of the world's children into one little sleigh.

The answer is not as complicated as you may think. I have help. As you learned earlier, my toy sacks are made from the magic cloth given to me by the Elves, which shrinks presents in size, in order to fit many thousands into one sack. My sleigh holds quite a few of these sacks, and groups of Elves fly with other reindeer teams to secret locations around the world to leave the next load of gifts for me to collect. When we first started, I would fly back to the North Pole to reload, but as the population grew and I had more deliveries to make, we soon realised that I would not have enough time for so many return journeys. I can reveal that one of the places I stop to reload each year is a secret spot near the peak of Mount Everest. I am comfortable revealing this location, as it is unlikely anyone will ever be there on Christmas Eve!

So, Christmas Eve is more of a team effort than perhaps you thought. The Elves fill the sacks up with presents, in the order of the houses I will visit, according to that year's route plan. This means I can move quickly from one house to the next. The Elf and reindeer teams then meet me along the route at these strategic locations, in order to save me more time. The sleigh and the reindeer do all the flying and I simply deliver the gifts.

29

Conclusion

I have been extremely fortunate to watch the growth of humanity over hundreds of years and to have seen so many remarkable developments. These changes have proven to me that the future is always full of hope and promise.

The Elves have been great teachers, from whom I have learnt so much. Although their way of life may seem at times quite simple and uncomplicated, we can all learn something from the way that they live their lives and see the world around them. Their ancient knowledge and long lives have been brought about through their mastery of time. They see it as circular, with no beginning, middle or end, believing that, like all life, it is connected to a never-ending cycle. It is this knowledge that, in part, helps me to deliver presents to all of the world's children on Christmas Eve. More importantly, this wisdom helps give them a greater understanding of the world. They know that each and every moment holds unbounded potential and that, at all times, anything is possible. This seems to be the source of their constant hope and joy.

The Elves have told me that it is their wish for all of us to try looking at the world around us with a more open mind. If you find Elven magic hard to believe, then perhaps try to imagine how things more familiar to you, such as aeroplanes, television, the Internet and mobile phones, may have appeared to your ancestors, just a few hundred years ago. If you think about it, magic is not too dissimilar to science. It is simply based on a more ancient understanding of the laws of nature and the world around us.

As I mentioned earlier, the Elves have always known that the children of today will build the world of tomorrow. It has always been their dream that

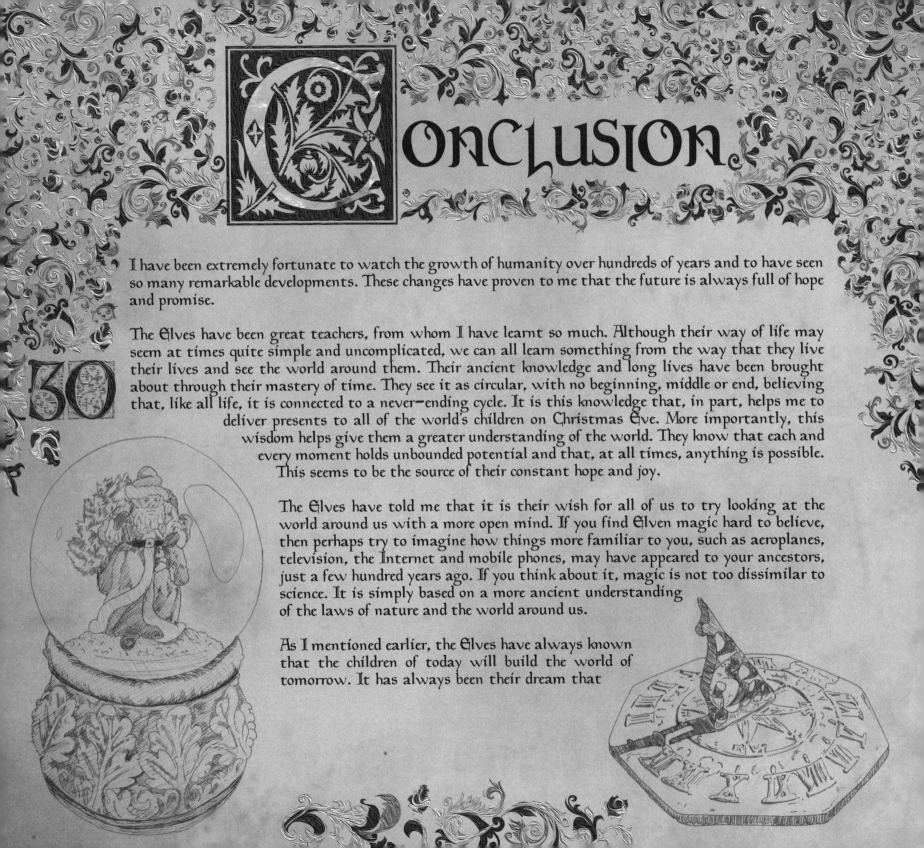

by helping children, they may be able to help the entire planet. Because of their love for all living things, they and myself will always try to help when and where we can. As you know, we watch over the children of the world and always try our best to provide help for those in need. As I explained, we have helpers who report back to us, but there is another way for us to see what children are doing. This is through the use of our magic glass viewing balls. We pick up the ball and shake it, and it shows us exactly what a child is doing at that very moment in time. Sometimes the picture is not very clear and gets interference, like bad tuning on a television set. It is likely that this is where the idea for snow globes originated from.

I feel that it is right for me to add that, whilst the year glass records the balance of the good and bad things that you do throughout the year, it should not only be the promise of presents at Christmas time that determines whether you choose to be naughty or nice. It is important for you to understand that being nice, doing good things and helping people will make good things happen to you all year round. For every good thing that you do, something good will happen to you. The more people that do good things, the happier people will be and when people are happy they make those around them happy. This means that happiness is able to spread endlessly, making the world a much better place.

I hope that you have enjoyed reading this book. I would like to wish you, your friends and your family many merry Christmases to come.

Santa Claws

Santa's
World Map
1789